Persistence

The Power & Breakthrough of Fervent Prayers

U. M. Hiram

D2R Management Group LLC
Junction City, Kansas

Persistence: The Power & Breakthrough of Fervent Prayers (Merry Hearts Inspirational Series Book 8)

Copyright © 2021 by D2R Management Group LLC. All rights reserved.
www.authorumhiram.com
Edited by Janice M. Allen: www.janicemallen.com
and Lissa Woodson: www.naleighnakai.com
Cover Designed by J. L Woodson: www.woodsoncreativestudio.com
Interior Designed by Lissa Woodson: www.naleighnakai.com

ISBN 978-0-578-93819-6 (eBook)
ISBN 978-0-578-93919-3 (Paperback)

Persistence

The Power & Breakthrough of Fervent Prayers

U. M. Hiram

"I can do all things through Christ which strengtheneth me." (Philippians 4:13, KJV)
To those who are facing challenges in your life and think there is no way out, I encourage you to trust and believe in the power of fervent prayers. The heartfelt, soul churning pleas for change and release from whatever situation has you feeling down and hopeless. Know that there is a greater power at work on your behalf. Faith is the key to unlocking the blessings tailor made just for you. As a living witness to overcoming many of the tough situations in my life, I know that you will too. Be confident in the amazing power of the Heavenly Father.

＊ ACKNOWLEDGEMENTS ＊

First and foremost, I want to thank God for allowing me to be on this phenomenal literary journey with an amazing array of talented authors. Writing has been a part of my DNA for a very long time, whether crafting a poem, journaling my private thoughts, or writing lyrics to a song. Unexpected life changes shifted my focus and the pen rested from my hands for a number of years. The creativity never wavered, just took a brief pause.

It's truly amazing to live in the power of divine order. Naleighna Kai, I appreciate you for being obedient to the calling of putting this inspirational series together. You are tough as nails, but such a tremendous blessing to those who are fortunate enough to be placed in your path. An amazing teacher, cheerleader, and savvy leader. I've been gaining so much knowledge from you and I'm thankful to be on this journey with you.

Janice Allen, it was a pleasure to work with you during the line editing process. You are great at what you do and thank you for the nuggets. It's sometimes daunting to think about someone else looking over your work and anticipating their thoughts. You did it with grace and wisdom.

Creative extraordinaire J.L. Woodson, you are a magnificent designer. I love and respect the way that you approach the book cover design process. All of your hard work and those keen eyes prove over and over again how extremely talented you are, and I want to thank you for all that you do.

Jenise, Brandon and Malcolm, you already know that you are my rocks and foundation. Thank you for making me laugh when I wanted to cry and pushing me to be the best version of myself. Your patience and understanding of me having to be in the writing cave on several occasions is appreciated. I love you all with everything in me.

Last, but certainly not least, The Tribe Called Success. Every one of the women and men in this family of creatives are phenomenal talents. Thank you for embracing, encouraging, and supporting me on this journey. Great things are on the horizon and I'm extremely proud to be in this community of rock stars.

U. M. Hiram

Her hands speak of long hours, distant shores and lullabies unsung. The lifelines meandering across her palms reminisce over passions pursued and grief that overflows. Time left its mark as indelible as fingerprints. Trust and kindness became myth, and detours made the path—and perhaps the climb—far steeper than imagined. But then she reached the top with hands scuffed from the journey and a heart filled with new scars that shimmer with seams of gold. With hands wide open, bitterness and resentment spill away as The One that loves her most restores what the locusts devoured. Grace and mercy shimmer in her hands as a new chapter unfolds.

— Stephanie M. Freeman, *author of* Unfinished Business *and* Nature of the Beast

Chapter 1

One man, two wives.

Children laughed and played outside under the clear, sunny skies of Ephraim; a small town located thirteen miles northeast of the capital city of Jerusalem. Hillsides served as a backdrop for their mischief. Adolescent young men were playing tag, throwing rocks, and wrestling one another. Their liveliness filled the atmosphere, while the young ladies sat nearby admiring their own simple, beautiful attire and watching the action.

Enjoyable and sometimes nerve-wracking sounds traveled throughout the courtyard. They served as constant reminders that one woman was able to provide her husband heirs, while the other was not. A daunting, heart wrenching experience. Elkanah, Hannah, and Peninnah shared a life, but they were not parallel. The scale was visibly unbalanced. A continual reminder of a seemingly unanswered prayer.

How could anyone coexist in this space?

Resentment, disappointment, strife, and envy were sure to reside—and they did.

Hannah's desires went beyond what her husband provided. Beautiful and favored by Elkanah, she was well taken care of, lacking for nothing. Yet longing for one precious gift. They loved each other, but it pained her tremendously that no child had been conceived between them. A woman's worthiness was attached to the number of children she was able to provide to her household. Hannah was failing miserably in that aspect.

Despite this, Elkanah showed her favor. Double portions, extra affection, and the utmost respect in spite of her childbearing difficulties. She was a striking woman with shoulder-length black hair and flawless skin. Penetrating brown eyes bore into your soul, and her figure fueled as well as satisfied her husband's desire.

None of this was enough to bring contentment to a barren woman yearning for a child.

Deciding to take a walk around the grounds, Hannah covered herself and headed towards the front entrance. As soon as she made it outside, she looked to her left and found her nemesis—Elkanah's second wife Peninnah—sitting there. It seemed today the entire household wanted to get out and enjoy the beautiful weather. Before she could turn in the other direction, Peninnah stood and walked boldly in her direction.

Bracing herself for the unwelcome interaction, Hannah silently took a deep breath. She wasn't scared of this woman by any means. She merely desired to be left alone and not antagonized. Silently praying, she refused to allow this woman's festered unhappiness to upend her peacefulness. Determined to keep a neutral posture, Hannah stood strong and didn't flinch when her space was invaded by the unwanted presence.

"Where are you heading? Are you finally leaving us?" Peninnah demanded. Her posture was adversarial, her tone full of malice. Every time she opened her mouth, the surrounding air became stagnant. No greeting, just straight to an episode of bullying. Happiness seemed to evade this woman.

"And why would I be leaving my home?" Hannah replied calmly.

"Your home?" she spat. "I think the presence of me and my children are the only things making this place a home for Elkanah."

"Considering I was here and settled before you arrived, this is and always will be my dwelling place."

Peninnah rolled her eyes, saying "You're childless and taking up space. While you may do your best to keep Elkanah satisfied in other ways, there's one main area you're lacking in. So again, why are you here?"

The second wife often ridiculed Hannah, belittling and antagonizing her at every given opportunity. She was a constant thorn in Hannah's side. Feeling superior to Hannah, Peninnah felt it was her right to be an oppressor. Her jealousy was swift and deadly, like a speeding freight train.

Why?

It was obvious she felt she'd proven her worth as a woman. After all, she was the one who'd given their husband ten sons and two daughters. She alone was ensuring that Elkanah's bloodline continued on strong. On the flip side of that, Peninnah did feel envious that kindness and unconditional love was shown to someone she felt wasn't worthy of those honors. Wrath and animosity saturated the heart of Hannah's adversary.

The woman's voice was annoying. She was a nuisance who sucked up the air in her occupied space. Continuous hatred seeped from her pores. Peninnah was a beautiful landscape on the outside. Darkness and strife claimed residence internally.

Hannah was aware of her own beauty, but never flaunted it. She was modest in nature and kind to everyone. It appeared her warmth didn't do much to foster a peaceful existence with Peninnah. The woman was ruthless and unsympathetic to Hannah's plight.

"Did you not hear me?" Peninnah spewed venomously. "I asked you a question."

Looking at the woman as if she'd lost all her marbles, Hannah didn't respond, knowing this was the onset of a browbeating session. This woman pushed all of her buttons. But never wanting to carry hatred in her heart, Hannah wouldn't lash back; she'd just turn her feelings inward.

"I know you understand me. What's the matter? Are you going to cry again?" Peninnah snickered.

Taking a deep breath, Hannah replied smoothly, "I belong here as much as you do. Let me remind you again, I was here first and will remain for a very long time. So, you can think on that and continue to be your wonderful, hate-filled self."

She did her best to stay positive. Her faith was unbreakable, her prayers precise. Trusting God to change the current circumstances is what she kept holding on to. However, dire sadness and disappointment would appear when Hannah was painfully reminded of her infertility.

An arched eyebrow and wicked grin preceded the poison escaping her foe's lips. "Really? Well now. Remember this: you haven't even produced one heir for our husband," Peninnah laughed. "It's taken a second wife to accomplish what you should have by now. So, you think about that."

Verbal punches flowed from her mouth like the steady flow of a river. This woman knew no boundaries, except as it pertained to the right time to strike. Always when their mate was not around, and Hannah's vulnerability was obvious.

"Elkanah loves me," Hannah spoke in a whispered tone. Though a strong, painful indicator of her angst threatened to fill her eyes, she did her best to keep up a brave face. "Is that what pains you and the reason you're so nasty towards me?"

"You are here on borrowed time. Our husband needs children, and that's the one thing you aren't able to give him," she said, placing a hand over her stomach. "My womb has been blessed. Why has the God you pray to so often punished you?"

In that moment, Hannah's spirit took a huge blow. As much as she tried to let harsh words roll off her shoulders, it was a tough thing to do. The hurt and shameful feelings surfaced quickly. Her emotions took hold.

The evil comments always caused her grief. Suffocating, self-inflicted thoughts of feeling inadequate as a woman and wife pushed her into a depressive state. Her peace was disrupted by the hostility shown courtesy of the other woman sharing her living accommodations. Though at times it was unbearable, Hannah's faith was shaken but never wavered.

Despair filled her heart. Elkanah never made her feel less than a woman. However, Peninnah was a visual reminder of what was missing in her life. Regardless of the unpleasant words spilling from this woman's mouth, Hannah stood firm in her belief that she would be blessed with a child. Hannah felt deep down the God she served was powerful and would prove that by performing a miracle in her life.

"He isn't punishing me. It has not been my time, but that day is coming. Elkanah and I will have a child," she replied adamantly.

Peninnah laughed hysterically. "Yeah, right. I think when you're old and shriveled up, you'll still be talking about the same blessings that'll never come. Face it, you are not worthy. The sooner you embrace that fact, the sooner you can move on and out."

"Your evil words will come back to haunt you. My blessings will come, and you'll be a witness despite what you're spewing."

Another round of wicked words sent Hannah into a tailspin.

She turned and hurried hastily to her chambers, not allowing tears to escape her eyes.

As much anger as she felt about the wicked things Peninnah said to her, Hannah knew that praying would keep her from laying hands on that woman. Although her humbleness was seen as weakness, a fire burned inside. If unleashed, some external damage control would be needed. Her goal was to be the bigger person, not to react to negativity.

Entering her chambers, Hannah allowed herself to release the exasperation she'd been feeling. Salty tears flowed and the weight of sadness released from her soul. The human side of her battled with giving in to the anger and doubt, while the Spirit encouraged her to stand strong and keep the faith.

Food was brought to her during this time of solitude. Hours later, the sliced lamb, mixed vegetables, and baked bread were cold and untouched. The chambermaids came to take the food away, but left empty-handed, looking deeply concerned about her well-being. Few words were spoken, which was unlike their normal interactions. Hannah knew they would relay this to Elkanah, and it would only be a matter of time before he showed up to her chambers.

Chapter 2

As much as she wanted to appear unbothered, it was difficult to do. Her heart was aching heavily, feeling a massive weight of sadness.

Hearing the chamber door open, Hannah didn't move from the area she'd been occupying near the window. Her silent prayers had been interrupted, but she expected that to be the case, considering her actions. Right now, misery replaced her joyful nature.

"My love, what is troubling you?" her husband asked.

She felt his presence as he walked into the room but wasn't ready to turn around and face him. Hannah knew as soon as she did, Elkanah would be upset. It wasn't her intent to make him feel bad. Their love was strong, but the stress of infertility was taking its toll.

The tears streaming down her face could not be hidden from him. The untouched nourishment and Hannah's current appearance would worry him. Her despair was overwhelming and on full display.

She felt him walk up behind her. As soon as he placed both arms around Hannah, she sighed and cried even harder. Finally, Elkanah turned her around to face him.

"Hannah, why are you weeping, my love?" he queried, his gaze sweeping over the tray of food. "And why are you not eating?"

Her mouth opened slightly, but nothing came out.

"What is keeping you from being happy right now?"

Cupping his wife's face, he gently kissed her drenched face and lips. Hannah felt his love in the depths of her soul, but felt unworthy of it. All of the negative and painful things said to her earlier stayed at the forefront of her mind.

"What is it? Do I need to have a word with Peninnah again?" Elkanah questioned, his displeasure apparent.

"No, please don't," she finally whispered. "I'll be okay."

"Are you sure? I despise seeing you like this. You are much too beautiful to be this sad."

She didn't want Elkanah to think her affection for him wasn't real. Right now, Hannah was caught up in her feelings. Desperately wanting to have a child of her own; a reflection of her and the man she adored.

Looking up into her husband's eyes, she wasn't able to formulate any words. Anguish filled her, but she still quietly prayed, believing one day soon what she was asking for would manifest.

Hannah searched Elkanah's eyes as her tears began to dry up. Her protector, warrior and love continued to hold on. She reached up, stroked his face then kissed him; drawing strength and comfort in this moment.

No one mattered except the two of them. Hannah held on to her husband tightly. She needed this connection with him as a reminder of how true their love was for one another. Despite their current battle, it was evident their lasting relationship wasn't superficial or contingent upon anyone else's expectations.

Remaining in the chamber for a few hours, the couple connected physically and mentally. Laying in his protective arms, she relaxed and all the stress from earlier in the day became a distant memory. Elkanah asked the chambermaids to stay away the rest of the evening. Hannah was appreciative.

"Are you ready to eat, my love?' he asked, affectionately.

Snuggling into his chest, she replied, "Yes, I am."

"Okay, I'll get you a freshly cooked meal."

"That means you'll have to get up and leave," she playfully pouted.

Kissing her forehead, Elkanah rose from the bed and placed on his silk robe.

"I'll be back shortly, and we will get you fed properly."

Watching her husband leave, Hannah smiled and felt extremely loved. His attentiveness, patience, and protection of her heart meant the world. Once again, she felt a sense of peace and confidence in believing that their prayers would be answered soon.

Thirty minutes later, Elkanah returned with lamb, vegetables, bread, and fruit. Glasses filled with wine were also on the tray. Hannah looked as her husband arranged their meals on the small bedroom table. After filling their famished bodies, the couple talked and then prayed before going to sleep.

"I will lift up mine eyes unto the hills, from whence
cometh my help. My help cometh from the Lord,
which made heaven and earth."
(Psalm 121:1-2 KJV)

Chapter 3

The time for the family's trip to Shiloh was drawing near. Every year they'd travel as a unit to the area to pray and offer sacrifices in the Tabernacle. One day Hannah went to pray by herself after attending a gathering with her husband.

No one was inside the Tabernacle. She was able to be in solitude, surrounded by God's presence and focused on having her prayer answered. She was relentless in her petition to God for a child. Deep belief and trust in the Heavenly Father fueled her passion for praying fervently with high expectations.

"Oh Lord, heal me from this affliction", Hannah, wept loudly. "Father, if you grant me the desires of my heart and bless me with a child, I promise this blessing will be given back to you. This request is not in vain. Bless me, O Great God." The Holy Spirit came upon her as she continued to make her purposeful plea.

Deep in prayer and trusting God would grant her heart's desire, she made her petition to heaven. As the sound left her vocal cords, only her lips moved. No words, just silent unwavering faith. Engrossed in worship, she didn't hear the priest enter.

"What is wrong with you, woman?" Eli's stern voice sounded. "Are you drunk with wine?"

Taken aback by the accusation, Hannah stared blankly. She wasn't intoxicated at all. Interestingly enough, she was baffled this man of the cloth would allow those words to escape his lips. She maintained her composure during their interaction, although she felt slightly insulted.

"I am not drunk. My soul is grieved," she explained.

Eli gazed intensely at Hannah, as though assessing the truth of her words. His first assumption was she'd been drinking heavily because it appeared she was talking to herself. Instantaneously, his spirit was touched once he realized her soul ached.

"Why is your heart heavy, my child?" he whispered, moving closer to the candelabra.

"My soul is crying out to God because I'm believing Him for a miracle."

"Do you believe with everything in you that the Almighty will grant your petition?"

"I do, and I trust in His timing," she said adamantly. "My prayers are not futile."

"If you truly believe and trust our Heavenly Father, I stand in agreement with your appeal."

Eli spoke prophetic blessings over Hannah's divine appeal. She left with a victorious calmness.

One night after returning from the Tabernacle, during her lovemaking with Elkanah, she became pregnant with their first son. He was named Samuel, which in Hebrew means "God Heard." His birth was a joyous time, serving as evidence of how fervent prayer and faith works together.

Protective as a lioness over her cub, Hannah made sure her child was never in harm's way. She was especially diligent around Peninnah and her tribe of children. Some of them mimicked their mother's attitude and actions. Eye rolls and snide remarks were a daily occurrence. Elkanah was just as mindful and dutiful about being a shield for his wife and newborn son.

As much as she trusted her maidens, Hannah wouldn't allow them to care for Samuel alone. Knowing God's protection surrounded them, she was at peace, but forever watchful. Loving the gift of this little human being was something indescribable.

"How's my beautiful wife and son doing today?" Elkanah chimed upon entering the chambers.

"We are doing well, husband," she smiled.

Hannah was breastfeeding Samuel, adoringly looking down at him. Tilting her head slightly, her husband kissed her cheek, showing his gentle affection. They both watched the miracle in front of them.

"He's strong and handsome like his father," Hannah said.

"We are blessed and I'm thankful to God for answering this prayer for us." Elkanah smiled brightly.

"I agree, my love, and I'm overjoyed that both of you are in my life. Our Heavenly Father is indeed faithful." Hannah looked into her husband's eyes as he leaned forward to place a gentle kiss on her lips. Nothing could spoil this moment for them because it was a dream come true.

Meanwhile, Peninnah was seething with envy. Feeling slighted, she was disappointed because Elkanah didn't spend a lot of time with her or their children. His attention was primarily on the newest edition to the family. Her sense of supremacy turned into self-doubt.

Never giving her adversary a second thought, Hannah was basking in the happiness of motherhood. Her son's temperament was peaceful and joyful. He didn't cry much unless hungry or needing to be changed. Samuel's presence had a calming effect in his environment. He was an observant baby. They doted on him because he was their miracle child.

Each of his days was filled with agape love. As he transitioned from infancy to the toddler years, she knew their time together would be limited. She had every intention of fulfilling the promise made prior to his conception.

As vowed, once he was weaned, Hannah took Samuel to the Tabernacle in Shiloh as a symbol of him being given back to God. She wanted to make sure her heavenly covenant was not broken. The tears and prayers would mean something for the living, breathing reminder gifted to her. Never struggling with her decision to make good on her promise, she was at peace with it.

When Hannah saw Eli, she said, "Good Priest, I am the woman who was crying out to God for a miracle. Alas, here is the blessing I've been given. In turn, I present his life to our Heavenly Father."

"Indeed, God is faithful, and you have made Him glad," Eli said, touched by her conviction.

"That makes my heart glad. I'm also at ease with the fact Samuel will be here in your care. He will grow up doing God's will and his covenant will be strong."

"You don't have to worry, my child. This young man will do great things. He is favored and blessed."

"And for that mere fact, I'm grateful and forever indebted to our Creator."

"Daughter, obedience and faithfulness will provide blessings upon blessings in your life."

Hannah did not feel any remorse, for she knew Samuel would be covered in protection. She'd miss seeing him every day, but knowing her son had a greater prophecy to fulfill calmed her spirit. Elkanah's deep faith allowed him to be in agreement with his son remaining with the priest.

Eli spoke prophetically over Hannah's life as she returned to the Tabernacle year after year. As a reward for her obedience, God opened her womb five more times. She and Elkanah were blessed with three more sons and two daughters. The power of prayer, faith and belief proved themselves to be true.

Meanwhile, as the years passed, Samuel continued to grow into a strong, faith-filled young man. The main purpose instilled in him and cultivated from an early age was to serve God. His mother's prayers were powerful. She kept her divine promise, and Samuel's predestined path was being brought to fruition.

His prophetic insight grew exponentially, and his gifts were instrumental in navigating through life. Receiving revelations through dreams, providing intercessory prayers, being positioned as a judge, then anointing King Saul the first sovereign over the nation of Hebrew people. All of this occurred from his mother's simple act of faith and fulfilling the promise she'd made to God.

"Ask, and it shall be given you; seek, and ye shall find; knock, and it shall be opened unto you. For every one that asketh receiveth; and he that seeketh findeth; and to him who knocketh it shall be opened."

(Matthew 7:7-8 KJV)

Chapter 4

This scripture displays the epitome of how powerful fervent prayer can be in our lives. When going through different phases of our existence, it is the one thing that can keep us centered and focused on the fact there is a greater power at work. Although we may not see immediate results, believing and pressing forward will allow those prayers to manifest.

Another profound revelation found in the story of Hannah is that making a covenant with God can provide blessings that benefit more than just yourself. Generational favor can travel through your bloodline. All it takes is a small amount of faith. Especially when you may be dealing with doubt, frustration, and temporary blindness based on the difficulties in front of you.

Two things about Hannah's story resonated with me: her fervent prayer life and her way of dealing with a naysayer. She prayed without ceasing, even though it looked like the odds were stacked against her.

I remember a time in my life when labels were given out as often as snide comments. For example, I heard things such as "You have messed up your life" or "You'll never be able to do that." Those are tame statements compared to some of the negative talk that was used by people who claimed they loved me or should've had my best interest at heart.

Reflecting on those impressionable times in my life, that unkindness baffles me. How can someone or people who say they love and care about you be so cruel? Can you see the dysfunctional behavior associated with this?

In addition to this type of behavior, I dealt with those who thought they'd be able to predict the outcome of my future. Invisible crystal balls hid behind their eyelids and their primary mission was to act as a personal judge.

Have you ever been told what people think you can't do?

Were labels placed on you growing up?

Did your life take a different direction from where you'd envisioned?

How did life choices change the trajectory for you?

In youthful days, there are certain adults (i.e., parent, aunt, uncle, or mentor) that you may find yourself looking up to or aspiring to achieve their success. You think to yourself that's the type of life that you want to be living. It appears there are no worries and everything is done with ease.

Fast forward to when you grow up and reality hits like a ton of bricks. You begin to understand there's more to their story and particular journey. Some of them are not so great, and the assessment of your life starts taking shape.

Decisions are made, some good and some bad. Hopes and dreams fuel your desires for the type of life you envision, but one moment in time changes all of that. This happened to me in the early stages of my adulthood.

Asking God to sustain me through all of the transitions and milestones was consistent. Those fervent prayers brought an amazing village into my life.

Chapter 5

At the age of nineteen, I found myself pregnant and unsure of what the future held. Plans definitely changed, I'd originally pictured myself as a performing artist, a successful singer and actor. I'd always wanted to be a mom; however, I didn't think it would be that soon in life. But when certain precautions aren't taken and you find yourself "in love," then the outcome is evident. That was probably one of the scariest times in my life.

Wrapping my head around the fact that I'd be responsible for this living, breathing little person who would depend on me for everything was such a daunting reality. So many thoughts raced through my mind about how I would provide for my child. I wasn't sure if I'd ever go back to college and finish out a degree program. For the time being, higher education was put on the back burner.

Growing up in the projects of New York, I didn't want that same reality for my child. Don't get me wrong, my sister and I didn't want for anything despite the fact my mother had to use government assistance. We always had a roof over our heads, clothes to wear, and food to eat. To be honest, we had no idea we'd been living as a low-income family.

The main prayer prior to and after my son's birth was for me to be strong on this journey with him. I had seen how hard it was for my mother to navigate her way through motherhood without support from her husband. Unfortunately, their marriage faced some challenging times and they ended up separating while my sister and I were still young. One minute I had a father in the home, then in the blink of an eye that changed.

A change such as this has a huge impact on a child. As I look back over some of the decisions I've made in life, in particular when dealing with relationships, it's extremely eye-opening. Becoming a mother, especially at a young age, pushes you to embrace adulthood at a quicker pace. Now, I understand what "unconditional love" and selflessness truly mean.

A maternal instinct kicks in and makes you look at life and the world a whole lot differently. Selfishness is placed at bay and your thoughts are shifted to the gift you've been given. This responsibility is very scary, joyful, unpredictable, and exhilarating. Being able to embrace this stage in my life and knowing there was a higher power at work helped in this transition.

I was going to be in a similar situation of raising a child minus the marriage, the same circumstance my mother had found herself in. And I would be much younger going through it. During my pregnancy, I was grateful for the fact that support came in the form of my son's godparents. Admittedly, the relationship with my mother was contentious because she was unhappy about me expecting a baby.

Needless to say, once Malcolm made his entrance into the world, the relationship between my mother and I began to heal. It's amazing how much of an impact this little person made on every adult he came in contact with. He melted hearts and brought so much joy to those around him on both sides of his family.

Providing for him was one of the main reasons I decided to join the military. It would provide a steady source of income. A significant part of that was the fact that my family was full of veterans who served in all of the different branches. Missing a few firsts for my baby boy was unthinkable, but the reward was going to be much higher than what I was going to be giving up. At least in my mind, it was.

The separation from him for a little while was extremely hard. Struggling with the guilt of having to leave Malcolm in the care of my mother bothered me a lot. He served as a huge source of motivation for me to successfully complete boot camp. I would not quit, no matter what I had to endure to get to the finish line.

The overall plan was for him to join me as soon as I'd gotten settled at my first duty station in Virginia. However, the time right before leaving for boot camp in Orlando was pure torture. The good thing for me was he was so young. Even though I missed him taking his first steps, it was a blessing he would be able to remember all the times with me after that.

Asking God to sustain me through all of the transitions and milestones was consistent. Those fervent prayers brought an amazing village into my life. Malcolm became part of their families just as I did. No matter the duty station, we were blessed to be surrounded by some amazing people. Childcare was never a worry when I was scheduled for duty on the base or had to go to school or training.

Extended, non-blood related family members played a crucial role in Malcolm's life growing up. He was able to be around a close-knit group of people from all different backgrounds. Since I only did two active-duty tours, he spent time growing up in Virginia and Georgia. This allowed him to be able to spend plenty of time in South Carolina with both sides of his family.

Malcolm was always an easy-going child. Quiet, smart, and inquisitive. Being a military child piqued his curiosity about wanting to see different places and have fun experiences. One of the many things important to me for him growing up was the exposure to different cultures. Living in New York from birth through junior high school exposed me to many of these environments, giving me a different perspective about the way life could be viewed and experienced.

For example, my love of the arts grew after taking field trips to see shows on Broadway. This led to me taking drama and having the opportunity to capture a leading role in Pearlie. It was a junior high school production, but still a huge accomplishment.

Music was another facet of the arts exposed to me. I learned to play a number of instruments, including the clarinet, piano, and keyboards. Unfortunately, in 1985, when we moved down South those skills decreased because there weren't a lot of opportunities for me to do any of this at that time. It didn't change the fact that I had gotten the chance to learn and flourish for some time.

At times I had feelings of anger and disappointment because it appeared opportunities were taken away from me. Not having a choice, at the age of fourteen, about the move down South was disheartening. Moving to a place where learning was slower, and technology wasn't at the forefront was not something I wanted to do.

Learning to embrace the journey from youth to now has taught me much about mustering up inner strength, ignoring naysayers, and becoming more confident in using my gifts. For anyone who may have been or is currently struggling with these challenges, I offer these three points of advice to you.

First, be careful about who speaks over your life. Don't allow anyone to impart negative statements such as what you can't do or how they feel you should move forward in navigating day after day. Hindrances will prolong your process. Allowing negative talk into your ears can decrease or destroy confidence levels.

Second, know your worth and recognize you have unique gifts and talents. We are all individuals created to do some amazing things while we're here on earth. Despite your past or current circumstances, trust in the fact you're able to achieve great success as long as you exercise faith and remain optimistic in your abilities.

Third, trust in your predestined path and never waiver when challenges surface. Although no one truly knows the direction life will go, don't get caught up in all of the details. Shifting can come as naturally as breathing. Nothing is going to be perfect. Stop feeling as if it needs to be that way. Channeling those positive moments and things in your life are essential to combating the negativity.

"For the Lord God is a sun and shield: the Lord will give grace and glory: no good thing will he withhold from them that walk uprightly."

(Psalm 84:11 KJV)

Chapter 6

The fairness of favor can be a thorn in someone else's side when they feel you are undeserving of the blessings happening in your life. You would think people want to see you thrive and flourish. Unfortunately, that's not the case. Some individuals don't want to see you succeed. A lot of times, it's those who are close to you.

Disheartening thought, isn't it? Unfortunately, a realistic fact. One that is really difficult to grasp. Hurtful when it comes to those who you care about and feel should want you to succeed. It makes one ponder, what are some of the underlying causes for this type of behavior?

Three components causing this contention could be jealousy, stagnation, and unhappiness with themselves. Envy is the ultimate root of hostility because someone covets what you've earned due to your hard work. This shouldn't be the case.

They'd be able to attain some of those same things if they would simply put in the work.

It is baffling that people are happy and engaging as long as they feel you're on a level playing field. Sadly, the moment it appears you are excelling and exceeding beyond their comfort level, then they have a problem with you. Crazy way of thinking, isn't it? Why would someone not be happy for your triumphs?

Developing a trusting relationship with someone or a close-knit group of people isn't always easy. When there's been a previous hurt, the caution flag is fully waving. Blinders are off and everyone is deemed suspect. As soon as those walls are broken down and individuals allowed into your space, it takes a lot of courage to hope for the best.

Can you think back to a time when you've trusted someone and they ended up turning their back on you? In a relationship or partnership?

How did that make you feel? Dejected or vexed?

Did you close yourself off from trusting anyone? Or did you overcome and move forward from that particular situation?

Personally, I can think of a select few times where anger was at the forefront of my feelings. Trying to ignore someone's deception was very difficult. As maturity and wisdom set in, learning not to react adversely is the best course of action. Retaliating can make you feel vindicated in the short term; however, you have to keep in mind that karma is real.

Would you want your actions to come back full circle?

How would it benefit you to become an aggressor mirroring the actions of the individual who has done something wrong to you?

One story in the Bible that speaks to this type of scenario is Daniel. He was a trusted advisor and practiced treating everyone fairly and respectfully. However, there are those who grew jealous of his perceived status and plotted to derail his existence.

Daniel prayed fervently three times a day. His faith and relationship with the Almighty were strong. Always constant in his daily prayer life, he made sure to reverence God through these actions despite the opposition set against him.

"He thinks he is above us all," one scribe said. "Why is the king listening to anything Daniel has to say? We should be his trusted advisors and the only three providing guidance to him."

Nodding their agreement, two other men stood with scowls on their face, a representation of the malice edged in their hearts. Immediately, they formulated a plan to set Daniel up. Jealousy was driving them to push for an imminent demise of the person standing between them and their agendas. They wanted the King's ear and felt the only way to do that was move Daniel out of the way.

Based on advice from his scribes, King Darius incorporated a thirty-day law about punishment for anyone praying to God or another human being when they should be worshiping him. Being thrown into the lion's den would be the penalty for violating this new law. Those individuals knew Daniel wouldn't deter from his daily practices, so it became a waiting game for them and a path to his demise.

"Your Majesty, may we have a word with you?" the leader of the scribes asked.

King Darius gave them permission to speak.

"It troubles us to tell you Daniel has been openly praying, which is against the current decree. We believe an example needs to be made of him. He has to be punished for disobeying your order, King Darius." The foundation had been laid for carrying out their evil plot.

The gold themed throne room became extremely quiet. Each

of the advisors briefly glanced at one another, awaiting the King's final verdict. There was no way he would stray from his decree. He would be consistent with following the laws put in place.

"Are you sure of the accusations you're making against Daniel?" King Darius asked, clearly troubled.

"He prays with his windows open and isn't ashamed of doing so each day. The law is binding, your Majesty. Punishment must be invoked. Thirty days was ordered, your Majesty, and he couldn't follow those simple rules. No exceptions should be made for this man."

"Trust me, I know the law is binding," the ruler replied with a hint of aggravation. Something did not bode well with him about this. But he knew he'd have to follow through with the consequences of disobedience to this decree. It could not be repealed.

Troubled about what needed to occur, King Darius braced himself for the order that would pass his lips. No way of getting around a law he'd imposed at the recommendation of his advisors. Appearing weak and unable to lead was not an option, so he gave a command. "Guards, arrest Daniel for disobeying my decree and bring him here to be sentenced. Do not harm him. I'm sure he will not resist."

Externally he exuded strength, while internally his spirit was unsettled and a bit angered upon realizing what his advisors had done.

Daniel wasn't surprised when the guards showed up to his home. They escorted him to the high court. Upon acknowledgement of his offense and sentencing, he was then taken to the lion's den.

The anguished leader spoke these words to Daniel, "Thy God whom thou servest continually, he will deliver thee." (Daniel 6:16 KJV).

Fear didn't enter Daniel's mind or his being. His faithfulness and consistent prayers had led to him being granted God's goodwill.

Once the stone had been rolled over the entrance, darkness engulfed the lion's den. Yet calmness surrounded Daniel. He sat down, not the least bit worried about his current circumstance. Taking a deep breath and closing his eyes, he placed his back against the stone wall.

Normally when a person had been put into this death trap, the lions would be ready to pounce. However, the favor of God rested upon Daniel's life. The dangerous, large cats acted as if he wasn't even in their space.

When morning came, Daniel looked up at the guards and his appearance was still untouched. The lions hadn't made a move towards him. Their ferocious appetite had been curbed. His petitions to God were not in vain because he was a faithful servant.

King Darius' unsettling spirit had made him restless all night. Now, he felt at ease because he learned that his most trusted advisor was safe. He commanded that Daniel be removed from the lion's den expeditiously. Unfortunately for the men who had tried to get Daniel killed, the tables were turned.

"Take them all to the lion's den," the king ordered.

"Your Majesty, why are you condemning us to this fate?" the leader of the scribes asked.

A prolonged stare and sneer were clear indicators of the King's anger. His volatile state further ignited at the audacity of their false remorse.

"Dare you ask me why? Did you not conspire to have Daniel die in the lion's den?" King Darius roared.

"We brought it to your attention that he didn't follow the law you'd put into place. Why are we being punished? This is not our fault," the scribe stammered.

Dumbfounded, the other two men looked on nervously and in utter disbelief. Usually, they could think of a way to slither out of any mess. Not this time.

"You purposely pushed for this law because you knew Daniel was faithful in his prayer life," he replied. "Now, you will suffer the consequences of your actions."

Eyes wide with fear and sweat rolling down their foreheads, there was nothing that could be said to stop the inevitable. Unfortunately, they would pay for all of their unsavory deeds.

"But King Darius, we were only trying to make sure the laws were followed," they pleaded as one final recourse, doing their best to figure out a way of avoiding being punished. Begging for their lives and trying to make excuses were the last resort.

"No more," the King shouted. "May God have mercy on your souls. Guards, remove these men from my sight and make sure that their families join them. The lion's den awaits them all."

The conversation was dismissed, and an eerie silence took place as the guilty were fed to the lions. The animals took no time to devour those thrown into their lair.

With all of the scribes' evil intentions, it backfired. They and their families paid the ultimate price.

Chapter 7

There's an age old saying about digging a hole for someone: it might actually be for you. A true statement when you have evil intentions against someone. Fate is inevitable based on the actions of an individual.

Does this type of behavior sound familiar?

Did you ever have someone, or a group of people conspire against you?

Were there plots and plans you've felt were put in place to stop you from achieving your predestined goals?

It's difficult when you place your trust in the wrong people or give them more respect than what is given to you. Humbleness can take on a derogatory meaning, especially dealing with passive aggressive individuals. You try to do the right thing, but that can lead you into becoming too comfortable in an environment only meant to be for a season.

Life has a way of changing in an instant. One rollercoaster ride can be both exhilarating and exasperating. Facing tests is inevitable and our method of dealing with those will determine our outcome. Two of those personal moments in my life challenged me mentally. These instances should have broken my spirit; however, the power of prayer was my saving grace.

Over a couple of years ago, I was laid off from an employer where I'd worked faithfully for a number of years. It caused me to shift my thinking and realize that comfort-zone living is not ideal. This ordeal was probably one of the most difficult times of my life for a number of reasons.

First, my financial landscape was totally changed. As you find yourself being paid a decent salary, it can allow you to become comfortable. You get into a routine and feel as if there's nothing to be concerned about because you're looking forward to consistent income.

Second, the handling of this decision was hurtful because a few things were done behind my back. I was very aware the organization was having financial constraints; however, the message given to me was there would be discussions about how things would be handled. Unbeknownst to me, a sole leadership decision had already been made and was shared with other staff members.

Imagine being sent to training that would benefit the organization, then walking back into an uncomfortable space. Your world is turned upside down. Mental and physical strengths are tested.

Third, I was angry with myself for being loyal to a fault. In simple terms, feelings of betrayal surfaced. If this whole situation had been handled with respect and care, then I would have been fine. Change has never been a problem for me; however, the manner in which it was handled counted the most.

Empathy can go a long way when it comes to dealing with life-altering events. Being the bearer of bad news isn't the most ideal position to be in; however, the way in which you manage communications about it shapes the reactions to it.

Honestly, it took me a while to come to terms with the handling of this situation. However, I will be the first to admit that it was a blessing in disguise. While I don't regret being an integral part of that organization, it taught me some huge lessons about becoming too comfortable in a space.

Let's talk about the ultimate consequence of being laid off— no or reduced income.

Struggling with many thoughts running through my mind, many emotions were front and center because of the challenging financial shift for me. Unfortunately, my savings plan took a backseat because I was paying off debt and some unforeseen events had occurred. Imagine writing down a plan and gearing up to execute it, only to be sidetracked.

Did I feel frustrated? Yes, most definitely.

Issues with my vehicle left me no choice but to purchase a newer, used model. It wasn't in the plan to take on a monthly car payment since the current vehicle was paid off. Electric and eventual engine problems changed everything.

Now, just a couple of months later, my livelihood was taking a hit. Rent, car payment and other bills were at the forefront of my mind. Uncertainty about how long I'd be able to maintain based on income versus expenses became stressful.

Being placed in this position was very eye-opening for me. It made me face the fact that being expendable is real. Unfortunately, financial constraints happen, especially with small organizations, and you have to be prepared to deal with the unexpected.

Allowing personal feelings and emotions to stay at bay can be challenging. When you've devoted time, talent, and energy to an organization, it is clearly evident you are fully invested. So, for me, a number of questions ran through my mind because of this.

Why? Yes, I asked God this ultimate question. Growing up, I'd always been told we shouldn't make that inquiry. However, in my spiritual walk, having this type of conversation with my higher power was second nature to me.

Were there discouraging moments during this time? Indeed, there was a sense of feeling failure. Struggling with this can cause your self-esteem to waiver. Working to process what you could've done better, if anything, is something you ponder.

Was there a sentiment of anger? Yes. As much as I was trying to keep these emotions at a distance, it was difficult because everything was fresh. Honestly speaking, this provides a challenge because it takes time to switch your mindset from the cynical thoughts.

Feeling of bitterness creeping in? Absolutely.

I internalized a ripple effect of feelings. They eventually spilled over into my external moods. On top of that, once that employment was over, I was unable to receive unemployment; this only fueled the disappointment and betrayal I felt about that whole situation. Honestly, it took me a while to come to grips with the timing of everything.

Change is never an easy process. I've always been one to try to embrace it. However, in this instance, the difference was my life was altered in an undesirable manner.

Even in the midst of all that was happening, my faith didn't waiver about better days coming for me. Being a firm believer that things happen for reasons, sometimes beyond our control, is what helped me maintain through these dark moments. At the end of the day, I realized worse things could have happened, and I was thankful they hadn't.

One of the saving graces for me was that my sister and I had decided to consolidate down to one household. This turned out to be a blessing in the midst of this challenge. Some people don't have that option. I'm thankful I did.

It is my thought that God allowed this to happen to get my attention. When you pray about certain things, and you don't act when you are supposed to, the Heavenly Father has a way of shuffling things around in your life. This entire situation definitely made me take notice.

Although this was a tough time, God still provided for me, allowing a roof over my head, clothes on my back and the means to make an income. As a result of many prayers, I was hired for contract work in my field. That work led to being offered a part-time job, then eventually a full-time position.

All of this forces a shift of focus with the direction of my life's journey. I learned to appreciate the fact there was a huge amount of favor and blessings happening for me. It made me plan and execute some goals, which had been set aside due to schedules and being busy.

Consistently praying and trusting the spiritual journey proved invaluable. Many days were tough, but in the end, I was able to make it through. Fervent prayer and a small amount of faith is a powerful combination. No matter what comes your way or what life circumstances change, you can count on the fact that what you've been praying for will come to pass. Keep looking forward, have faith, and maintain your covenant with God.

Two other instances where prayer was a huge factor in sustaining my mental health was dealing with a few physical health scares. Being in good physical health, it was frightening to hear the doctor inform me about possible cancerous cervical cells, and on another occasion finding a lump in my left breast.

As you can imagine, both of those events weighed heavily on me. Honestly speaking, depression was on the verge of rising up. Though we try to keep a positive outlook on circumstances, there are some which pull on our human nature. At the end of the day, it can be hard not to look at what we're dealing with in real time versus the optimism of the situation.

For those who have been betrayed and hurt in any kind of way, I would offer three key areas of advice. These are things I've personally practiced daily. It isn't always easy to do but being intentional about them can keep you focused on the favorable aspects of life.

First, always remember there is a higher power at work on your behalf and you don't need to react to your betrayer. "The Lord shall fight for you, and ye shall hold your peace." (Exodus 14:14, KJV) Many times, the human side of us wants to retaliate because of the wrong done to us. It's our carnal nature. In younger years, this was a huge struggle for me because I wanted the person who hurt me to feel that same pain. Maturing and growing in faith totally changed my outlook. Now, if someone decides they want to treat me wrong, there's a calm space that I enter through prayer and patience. It's both liberating and empowering to learn that there's nothing you can humanly do that will compare to how God decides to deal with a person who has evil intentions against you.

Second, don't dwell on what was done to you because it can be kryptonite to your soul. The person or people who did something wrong to you will keep living their lives, not worrying about what their actions did to you. You have to be intentional about letting go of the hurt and anger. Granted, you never forget their actions, but you learn how to move past them and press forward in your present as well as towards your bright future.

Third, live your life to the fullest! Obtaining success in your endeavors is the sweetest retribution. When your attention is turned away from irrelevant people and focused on your goals, then that is one of the most peaceful spaces you can be in. No worries about anybody's next move, other than yours. Keep your overall goal in your eyesight and celebrate all milestones. Also, surround yourself with a small circle of compatible individuals to stay inspired.

One thing you can count on when you don't react to evilness, is your life will be blessed. This may sound cliché, but it's the absolute truth. The transgressors will not prevail in the end. They may experience temporary self-satisfaction for their deeds; however, you can count on the fact they will be accountable for all unpleasant acts committed against others.

Someone once sideswiped my car in the community we lived in. When it came time to file the police report, she changed her story instead of admitting fault because someone close to her advised her to do so. You already know I was angry and aggravated by the change in her demeanor. Although I wanted to react in an undignified way, divine intervention kicked in. Ironically, no more than two weeks later, one of their vehicles was totaled. In addition, the repairs to my vehicle were minimal, with no extra out of pocket costs.

This story may seem trivial to some, but it is a prime example of what can happen when someone doesn't have your best interests at heart. Maintaining your composure, even when you're tempted not to do so, can carry you a long way. While that person may feel they are getting away with something, the script can be flipped in an instant.

Evil deeds will always be punishable. Never be the one to feel you need to repay wrongdoing with your own type of vengeance. "Dearly beloved, avenge not yourselves, but rather give place unto wrath: for it is written, Vengeance is mine, I will repay, saith the Lord." (Romans 12:19, KJV) That scripture sums it up well.

Know there is a higher being at work on your behalf. If you believe, trust, and move yourself out of the way, those who conspire against you will be dealt with on a level that is way out of your own reach. Realizing you don't have to carry the weight of the world on your shoulders, especially when people attempt to do you wrong or are malicious, should bring you comforting peace.

"Now faith is the substance of things hoped for, the evidence of things not seen."

(Hebrews 11:1 KJV)

Chapter 8

Faith is defined as "complete trust in something or someone." Looking at circumstances and situations through human lenses can place you in a state of doubt. However, your spiritual belief will allow you to trust despite what things look like naturally. A higher power is at work on your behalf.

One biblical story speaking to this type of faith is about a Roman Army Commander. He knew Jesus was passing through the area and wanted to make a petition to Him. Believing and trusting in the power of the Lamb of God, he made an intentional decision to take a leap of faith.

On a sunny warm day near Capernaum, Jesus made his way towards the town after coming down from delivering a powerful sermon. Jewish elders met Him as He was making His way into the town, approaching Him on behalf of a Roman Centurion whose prayer was to have his gravely ill servant healed. This took a great amount of faith. The Savior was moved.

"Our Lord, we need your help," the elders earnestly pleaded. "A centurion's servant is at home, terribly suffering. Your healing power can make him whole. We are here on his behalf to make this humble request of you."

Even though a crowd of people were following Him after he came down from the mountainside, Jesus halted his steps upon hearing their plea. The Holy Spirit stirred within Him as confirmation that He needed to perform this miracle. Since the distance wasn't far to the home, Jesus decided to make the brief journey.

"I will come with you."

Those were the only words that He spoke, and Jewish elders led the way. Picking up more followers along the way, no one spoke out loud. They were on this journey to witness the wonder that would be performed.

Upon nearing the Centurion's home, a few of his close friends met Jesus and those traveling alongside. They'd been sent to stop him from entering the home. The Roman Army Commander felt he was unworthy to have God's Son enter his home.

The Centurion's message was, "Lord, trouble not thyself: for I am not worthy that thou shouldest enter under my roof: wherefore neither thought I myself worthy to come unto thee: but say in a word, and my servant shall be healed." (Luke 7:6-7, KJV)

Looking at the man's friends, in amazement, Jesus was touched by that shared declaration. It made His heart glad when pure, unadulterated faith was shown. He knew the centurion believed wholeheartedly in the power of the Almighty.

"He is a man of great faith," Jesus said. "I am touched by his immeasurable display of trust."

The crowd stood in astonishment, waiting in anticipation for what would happen next. Miracle after miracle was happening all around them in His presence. He turned to those following

Him and simply said, "I say unto you, I have not found so great faith, no, not in Israel." (Luke 7:9, KJV)

A moment later, Jesus turned back to the Centurion's friends and instructed them to go back to the home. An instantaneous, spiritual healing took place. Upon returning to the house, the gravely ill servant was found to be extremely well.

How amazing is that?

Having faith that strong in a divine power, then witnessing your prayers answered instantaneously. Trusting, believing, and knowing what you ask for will come to fruition. Even when things don't look like they are working in your favor or for your good, it's astonishing to know there's a godly order in place.

A number of biblical stories serve as an example of this powerful attribute. Sometimes there's a struggle to keep trust, especially when it feels like your world is falling apart. Trials will make it a challenge to keep moving forward and believing there are better days ahead.

However, when it has been proven to you over and over again there's a powerful force at work for you, then having faith is a given. Think back to situations where you could have been hurt or were saved from a possible catastrophe. Although we are given a choice to make decisions, there are times when they aren't necessarily the best ones.

While sometimes our prayers may turn out results opposite of what we may initially hope for, they are still answered. Many times, these outcomes are better for whatever the situation is you're facing. Even during those hard-faced moments, God is still controlling everything.

In times of sickness, strife, and even death, there's a higher power at work.

Death is something we know is inevitable. Truthfully, many of us would probably feel better if we didn't have to deal with this part of life's journey. Trying to compartmentalize and not question God is a struggle, especially when you lose someone close to you. There have been many deaths which have shaken me to my core. Two that challenged me the most were my mother and Uncle McArthur.

Watching a strong, beautiful woman with a heart of gold be strong while raising two girls, then have a mental breakdown, was tough to see growing up. My mother wasn't only loving to my sister and I, but to other children who were around her. She was protective, nurturing, and stern. Also, hilarious and could bake some delicious cakes and pies. That explains why there were folks wanting to come to our house to consume desserts on many occasions.

Over the years, even with battling mental and physical illness, mom was always trying to take care of others. It was hard going through these experiences with her. No one wants to see their loved one struggling and going through these types of difficulties. It can be taxing on a person. As her decline became more progressive, the decision had to be made to get assistance outside of the house.

Having to make the choice to place your parent into a facility is not made lightly or without concerns. You hear and see stories about elderly abuse. Fortunately, we were able to be engaged and it was helpful that my sister has a medical background along with personally knowing professionals who work in the field.

On May 9, 2017, my heart felt pain unlike anything it's ever experienced before in my forty-nine years on this earth. My baby sister received the call our mother had transitioned, and she had to be the one to tell me. When she first gave me the news, I don't think what she said to me even registered. All I knew was we needed to get to our mom. As the news began to sink in while I was driving, all kinds of emotions began to surface. Sadness, hurt, anger, and guilt.

Sadness and hurt were immediate. This is the phenomenal

woman who gave birth to me. She is the one who fought tooth and nail to do the best she could for her girls when our father was no longer in the household. Anger seeped in slowly as a result of me selfishly wanting her back here with us. Granted, she was on this earth with us for sixty-nine years, but it still didn't seem like enough time for me.

Finally, a huge feeling of guilt hit me. I was supposed to go see her but decided to wait until Mother's Day because I wanted to be able to enjoy that day with her. Little did I know, within one week, everything would change, and that chance would be taken away. Time is something we can never get back, a huge lesson learned for me.

When your intuition tells you to do something, listen and do it without pause. Especially regarding those we love and cherish. Whether it's making a phone call, going to visit, or even praying for that person. Life can be altered in the blink of an eye.

I operated on auto-pilot from that day until May 21, 2017, when we laid her to rest. Traveling back to South Carolina for this moment was heart wrenching. Mother's Day will always be bittersweet for me because that's around the time we lost her and because I was blessed to be a mother myself. It feels surreal at times to know we can't see her smiling face any more or I will never again be shaking my head at her sarcastic remarks. Even though my mother could be challenging at times, she had a heart of gold.

The memories of her baking cakes or cooking for others will forever be ingrained in me. I'll always remember listening for her to call my name before the streetlamps came on in our New York City neighborhood, or the boisterous tone when she was hollering my name down that long dirt road in South Carolina. Those moments will never be forgotten and laughter rises up in my belly when I recall those times.

My mother would always use that age old saying " as sure as

you live, you will die." A truthful and real-life statement. Not something we want to think about; however, it's inevitable.

Looking at her pictures, I can recall the events or holidays surrounding them. The memories are vivid and feeling her presence is an anomaly. Sometimes I've wished the mirrors weren't reflective, as her features are present in both of her daughters. It is unnerving sometimes that my sister and I have mannerisms identical to our mother's.

It's comical to think about being younger and expressing how different we were going to be from our matriarch. That is usually what many children share, but you mature and then the unthinkable happens. You find yourself using the same catchphrases your parent used, the very words that made you look at her as if she were an alien.

As daunting as that may seem, it is also comforting and keeps them close to you. Memorable moments etched in your mind. Laughter fills your soul when you have those moments of feeling sad and distressed.

Learning to deal with death and the grief that follows is an ongoing process. It always amazes me when people try to put a time limit on it. Everyone is different and it isn't fair to force an opinion on someone because of how you may feel. I'm a firm believer in not being handicapped by these moments but embracing them and finding your path to move forward and continue living.

Leaning on God as if my life depended on it was inevitable on this life's journey. Fervent prayer got me through those moments. Losing your mother places a hole in your heart that can never be replaced. A Bible verse that I turned to can be found in (Revelation 21:4, KJV). "And God shall wipe away all the tears from their eyes; and there shall be no more death, neither sorrow, nor crying, neither shall there be any more pain: for the former things are passed away."

At the end of the day, I know God allows things to happen even though we don't understand it. Death is definitely one of those aspects of life that's difficult to deal with, especially when it's someone so close to you. A piece of you feels as if it's missing and can't be replaced.

"To everything there is a season, and a time to every purpose under the heaven. A time to be born, and a time to die; a time to plant, and a time to pluck up what that which is planted."

(Ecclesiastes 3:1-2, KJV)

Chapter 9

The death of my Uncle McArthur was one of the worst days of my life, outside of losing my mom. He was one of my favorite uncles who I loved hanging out with and was always ecstatic about seeing when he got off the road from driving his eighteen-wheeler. Moving down from New York, it was so cool how our bond grew. He was one of my younger uncles and I respected him so much.

The day he lost his life in a trucking accident was such a devastating time for me. My grandmother was waiting at the school bus stop, and immediately my stomach dropped because I knew something was wrong before she even said anything to me.

I will never forget the grief-stricken expression and the words she spoke when telling me he had been killed in an accident. The rush of air leaving my lungs and standing in a state of shock is vivid for me to this day. He was just too young. He was getting ready to get engaged and it seemed as if his life was just suddenly ripped away.

So many emotions, so many thoughts at an impressionable age.

Why did this happen? What did he do to deserve this?

These two questions entered my mind. I didn't understand why he had to be taken that way. There was just so much more life to live and experience. I just wanted him back and wished everything was just a big old nightmare.

It took me a long time to come to grips with this. He was always larger than life to me. He was kind, with a sternness, protectiveness, and aptitude for making people smile. Every time that eighteen-wheeler rolled past our house, I got excited because I knew he was coming back to check in on us.

Looking down the dirt road in the direction of his house, my heart would break all over again. For the longest time, I didn't want to drive on the highway because I knew I'd have to share it with those trucks. The trucks that I grew to dislike for a while.

He worked hard, served in the National Guard, bought a house, and met a wonderful woman who he planned to marry. All of these positive things going on in his life, just to have it cut short. At that time, nothing would allow me to wrap my head around this tragedy.

Now many years later, how ironic is it that my son Malcolm has chosen this profession?

After school and training, the deal was sealed. He loves being able to climb in the truck and travel cross-country. The travel bug comes naturally because I instilled in him a desire to explore and learn new things.

Prior to him choosing to get behind the wheel of a rig, he served two terms in the Navy. Serving aboard an aircraft carrier and getting to see different parts of the world continued to fuel his passion for traveling. Having an uncle who used to be in this profession further motivated him.

Did this make me cringe? Just a little bit, but I'm a supportive and praying mother. Fervent prayer is powerful.

Does it make me think about Uncle McArthur? All the time. But making the choice not to dwell on what happened years ago has been intentional. A huge lesson with this is not to worry about what tomorrow brings, just to have faith God is orchestrating everything.

Reading and referencing one particular scripture helps with that balance. "Be careful for nothing; but in every thing by prayer and supplication with thanksgiving let your requests be made known to God ." (Philippians 4:6, KJV)

I send up prayers daily for my son's safety. No focusing on him traveling from coast to coast and thinking of the worst-case scenarios. Knowing he is covered spiritually is the best feeling in the world. Yes, that comes with growth and learning how to let go of things that are beyond our control.

Thinking about the what-ifs can cause you unnecessary stress. Focusing on the worst-case scenario isn't wise or healthy. We know each day should be cherished and spent making memories.

One of my favorite quotes is "life is not measured by the breaths we take but by the moments that take our breath away." It speaks to embracing life's most precious and memorable moments. Despite the low moments and challenges that we all inevitably must face, having faith and focusing on the positive is freeing.

Losing Uncle McArthur was such a huge loss and left a hole in my heart. Knowing death is a part of life does not make it any easier to accept or deal with. Prayer kept my mind from entertaining unsavory thoughts, allowing me to go through the grieving process but still come out strong. When loved ones transition, they will always be missed. However, we always have those memories to hold in our hearts. We have to find ways to move forward and on with life because I believe that's what they'd want us to do.

Lessons I've learned in coping with loss have proven to be of great comfort to me. Everyone has their own threshold for dealing with this valley of life. It's not one of our favorites, but a reality we have to face, nonetheless. Here are three ways I found to be helpful from day to day.

First, remember there's no time limit for dealing with grief. Don't let anyone tell you it should only take a certain amount of time for you to be over the loss of a loved one or someone close to you. The days, weeks, and years will begin to pass by—sometimes slowly and other times fast. No one has the right to tell you how to grieve or how long to grieve. "There is absolutely no time limit on grief, so don't rush yourself or let others rush you." - Unknown

Second, seeking support is great for your overall mental and physical health. One thing we have to remember is the person we lost has no further worries on this earth. Missing them is a given for those of us left behind; however, you have to think about how they would feel if we were to stop living life. Feeling overwhelmed and extremely sad are aftereffects of death. Prayer is huge, helping you to keep a sound mind. Other resources such as your pastor, a counselor or grief support groups can be great outlets to use, and these shouldn't be discounted. Don't let anyone make you feel bad or ashamed about wanting to reach out for this type of assistance.

Third, honoring your loved one's memory is helpful as well. How can you do that? Think about what causes may have been close to their heart and provide support through volunteerism or financially. For example, you can participate in a walk or day of service supporting mental health or breast cancer if either of those were important to the person you lost. Another avenue is becoming an entrepreneur and creating a non-profit organization that can bring awareness, raise funds, and help others who may be dealing with whatever illness your loved one dealt with.

Additionally, don't be afraid to talk or think about them often. Even though they are no longer physically present, it doesn't remove the memories you've shared. Pictures or videos are two other sources of keepsakes you can hold dear and near. Physically gone doesn't mean they should be forgotten or placed in a hidden box.

Learning to navigate through and deal with death, without being consumed by it, can help you to keep moving forward each day. Will it be an easy process? Of course not. Sadness and grief will be challenging, especially early on. But knowing your loved one isn't struggling or suffering should bring some comfort. Embrace the fact that they are at peace.

Ultimately, there is no perfect way to deal with loss. Praying for strength while going through the grieving process is at the top of the list. The higher presence in your life has the ability to provide comfort unlike any other. Even in your darkest moments of sadness, you can find relief in knowing that sunshine is just one season away.

About the Author

U.M. Hiram is an East Coast native who currently resides in Junction City, Kansas. She is an author, entrepreneur, human resource professional and retired Navy veteran. Her love for writing began at an early age, evolving into independent publishing years later.

She plans to write books in multi-genres such as contemporary fiction, inspirational, paranormal, and romantic suspense. In 2017, her romance fiction novel Finally was self-published and is set to be re-released soon. In 2021, two new releases are on the way from this author, Persistence and Queen of Wilmette.

Reading, traveling, watching sports and spending time with her family is what she enjoys doing the most when not putting pen to paper.

Website: https://authorumhiram.com/
Bookbub: https://bit.ly/UMHiramBookbub
Facebook: https://bit.ly/UMHiramFacebook
Goodreads: https://bit.ly/UMHiramGoodreads
Instagram: https://bit.ly/UMHiramInstagram
Amazon: https://bit.ly/UMHiramAmazon
Twitter: http://bit.ly/AuthorUMHiram

The Merry Hearts Inspirational Series will warm your heart
and touch your soul …

Milan Alessia Jackson battled through the scars left in her life from a contentious relationship. Her grandmother served as her protector and guardian angel until she took her last breath. International lawyer Vikkas Germaine was her childhood friend and true love. Life's circumstances separated them, but his father served as the catalyst to reunite them.

As the couple settle into their new marriage and Durabia, unexpected challenges rise up and threaten to tear their relationship apart. Secrets from her past, an unexpected trip to South Carolina and family members primed to settle scores surface, leading to a whirlwind of upheaval in their lives. Can their love survive these storms or will forces in play destroy everything they're building?

After four years, Michelle finally receives the marriage proposal a loyal and loving woman deserves. Michael Daniels was the man of her dreams and their relationship was both passionate and turbulent. So the trip to Montego Bay was a well-deserved vacation and surprise, and nothing could be more thrilling than to weather the storm and come out with a sunny day.

Until Michael's past catches up with him, derailing their short-lived bliss and ripping out the page of the next chapter in their lives. Destiny and happiness seem to take a backseat as they weather a new round of trials, challenges and hope to come out on the winning end.